Clifford THE BIG RED DOG®
Valentine Surprise

by Quinlan B. Lee
Illustrated by Steve Haefele

Based on the Scholastic book series
"Clifford The Big Red Dog"
by Norman Bridwell

No part of this publication may be reproduced in whole or in part, stored in a retrieval system, or transmitted in any form or by any means, electronic, mechanical, photocopying, recording, or otherwise, without written permission of the publisher. For information regarding permission, write to Scholastic Inc., Attention: Permissions Department, 557 Broadway, New York, NY 10012.

ISBN-13: 978-0-545-02845-5
ISBN-10: 0-545-02845-0

Designed by Michael Massen

12 11 10 9 8 7 6 5 4 3 2 1   8 9 10 11 12/0

Printed in the U.S.A.
First printing, January 2008

SCHOLASTIC INC.

New York   Toronto   London   Auckland   Sydney
Mexico City   New Delhi   Hong Kong   Buenos Aires

It was Valentine's Day.

Clifford and his friends were digging holes to hide their yummy valentine treats.

"Isn't Valentine's Day great?" Clifford asked.

"It's your kind of day," Cleo told him. "Big and red."

Clifford stopped digging.

He had to help Emily Elizabeth

deliver valentines.

"See you all later at the party," Clifford
called out.

T-Bone laughed. "Not if we see you first!"

Charley and Jetta were helping Emily
Elizabeth finish the valentines.

"I love Valentine's Day," said Jetta.

"Not me," Charley said, licking
another envelope. "It's too mushy."

"Are you coming to the party?" asked
Emily Elizabeth.

"All those hearts and lace," he said.
"No thanks!"

"Valentine's Day isn't only about that,"
Emily Elizabeth said. "It's about telling
people how much you care."

"Come with Clifford and me," said
Emily Elizabeth. "We'll show you."
Woof!
"I guess," Charley said.

The first card was for Sheriff Lewis.

It said: "Thanks for keeping us safe."

He smiled when he read it.

The next one was for Dr. Dihn.

Woof!

Clifford made that delivery extra special.

"Wow! Thanks!" she said, smiling. "That's the best—and wettest—valentine I've ever gotten."

They went all over the island
handing out cards.

And everyone who got one did the same thing:

They smiled.

"I'm glad there's only one left," said Emily Elizabeth.

"I have to get ready for the party."

Charley slid down Clifford's tail.

"Bye," he called. "I have to go!"

"Wait!" called Emily Elizabeth, but

Charley was gone.

That night at the party, everybody—and
every dog—was having fun.

Emily Elizabeth looked at her last valentine.

"I guess Charley really isn't coming," she said.

Just then, Charley walked in.

"You're here!" said Emily Elizabeth.

"I wouldn't miss it." Charley grinned.

"I just had to finish up something."

"Here." Charley gave two special
treats to Clifford and Emily Elizabeth.
"Thanks for showing me how cool
Valentine's Day really is," he said.

Woof!

"No problem," said Emily Elizabeth.

"Showing people you care is always cool."

"So did you deliver the last card?" Charley asked.

"Not yet," said Emily Elizabeth.

She handed Charley the last valentine.

"For me?" he said.

"Do you like it?" Emily Elizabeth asked.

"Like it?" said Charley. "I *love* it!"

Then like everyone else did . . .

He smiled.

Charley,
You're #1
in our
hearts!

Do You Remember?

Circle the right answer.

1. Why did Clifford stop digging?

   a. He had to help Emily Elizabeth deliver valentines.

   b. He was tired.

   c. He ran out of treats to bury.

2. Who was Emily Elizabeth's last valentine for?

   a. Dr. Dihn

   b. Charley

   c. Clifford

Which happened first?

Which happened next?

Which happened last?

Write a 1, 2, or 3 in the space after each sentence.

Charley came to the Valentine's Day party. _____

Clifford dug holes with Cleo and T-Bone. _____

Clifford, Emily Elizabeth, and Charley delivered valentines. _____